BILL COSBY

LITTLE BILL
BOOKS FOR
BEGINNING READERS

Money Troubles

by Bill Cosby

Illustrated by Varnette P. Honeywood

SCHOLASTIC INC.
Cartwheel
·B·O·O·K·S·®

New York Toronto London Auckland Sydney

Assistants to art production: Rick Schwab, Nick Naclerio

Library of Congress Cataloging-in-Publication Data

Cosby, Bill, 1937-
     Money troubles / Bill Cosby ; illustrated by Varnette P. Honeywood.
          p.   cm.— (A little Bill book)
     "Cartwheel books."
     Summary: While trying to raise enough money for a telescope, Little Bill makes a discovery about generosity and the needs of others.
          ISBN 0-590-16402-3 (hardcover)   0-590-95623-X (paperback)
          [1. Moneymaking projects — Fiction. 2. Generosity — Fiction. 3. Afro-Americans — Fiction.]
          I. Honeywood, Varnette P., ill. II. Title. III. Series. IV. Series: Cosby, Bill, 1937- Little Bill book.
PZ7.C8185Mo   1998
[Fic] — dc21   97-34106
                                                                                              CIP
                                                                                              AC
10 9 8 7 6 5 4 3 2 1   8 9/9 0/0 01 02

Printed in the U.S.A.   23
First printing, June 1998

To Ennis,
"Hello, friend,"
B.C.

To the Cosby Family,
Ennis's perseverance against the odds
is an inspiration to us all,
V.P.H.

Dear Parent:

One of the best ways children learn about the value and significance of money is through regular saving. Even small children appreciate the purpose of saving when they can buy toys with money from their piggy banks.

Eventually, children realize that *working* brings in money. To reinforce this important feature of the real world, some parents pay young children to do chores around the house as well as give them an allowance. Many parents, to discourage materialism, also encourage their children to donate some small amount of their savings to good causes.

Older children, like Little Bill, find they can also earn money through jobs outside the family. In *Money Troubles*, Little Bill is inspired to buy a telescope after learning about astronomy in school. (Not, it must be said, because he's suddenly become a serious scholar. Instead, he dreams of becoming famous. He'll discover a new comet, and it will be named after him.) The telescope he wants costs $100; he has $47.87 in his bank. To start earning the rest, he washes a neighbor's car, then collects cans and bottles—until he notices another boy, obviously poor, also out scavenging. Little Bill leaves his own cans where the other boy will find them.

Little Bill has realized something important: other people may need money more than he does. He takes this lesson further by dropping the telescope idea, donating all his savings to the school's food drive for the poor…and becoming "famous" for contributing the most food.

Through his unselfish acts, Little Bill has learned that giving to others can be more satisfying than acquiring a possession he can do without. And he has taken an important step toward understanding what it means to be part of a community.

Alvin F. Poussaint, M.D.
Clinical Professor of Psychiatry,
Harvard Medical School and
Judge Baker Children's Center,
Boston, MA

Chapter One

Hello, friend. My name is Little Bill and I am going to be famous. I'll tell you why. Do you want to know what I like to do? I like to look at the night sky. I do!

Way out there — way past Pluto — is the Oort Cloud. It looks like a cloud because it is made up of billions of comets. Billions.

My teacher, Miss Murray, said so. And she said maybe one day, one of those comets will pull away from the Oort Cloud. It will travel through space toward the sun.

And one day, when I'm looking up at the sky, I'll see that comet. And maybe I'll be *the first person ever* to

see that comet. I'll run and call the
people who give names to comets.
I'll tell them my name and what I
saw.

Then they'll say, "Congratulations!"
And they'll name it Comet Little Bill.
I'll be famous! Yessss! But first, I need
a telescope.

Chapter Two

I was shooting hoops in the driveway. Ms. Hernandez, our mail carrier, came by.

"I'll take it, Ms. Hernandez," I said.

There were lots of letters for Mom and Dad, a magazine for my brother Bobby, and some catalogs.

On the back of a catalog, I saw what I wanted — a telescope.

There was one *big* problem. It cost $100! Mom and Dad would never give me $100! There was only one thing for me to do. I had to get the money myself.

I already had some money in my football bank.

Some of the money was from Aunt Martha. She gave me a dollar when she came for a visit.

"Spend it wisely," she said.

Some of the money was from Uncle Joe.

"Enjoy it," he said.

Some of the money was from the tooth fairy.

I opened a little door on the bank and shook it. All the dollars, quarters, dimes, nickels, and pennies dropped out. An old stick of gum fell out, too.

I counted 34 dollar bills, 21 quarters, 53 dimes, 39 nickels, 137 pennies — and 1 old stick of gum.

I added all the dollars, quarters, dimes, nickels, and pennies. It took a long time. I had $47.87. I only needed $52.13 more and I could buy my telescope. I only needed $52.13 and I could be famous!

Chapter Three

On Saturday morning, I dressed quickly. I ran to the kitchen.

"What's the rush?" Dad asked.

"I have to get a job," I said.

Dad laughed. "What else is new?"

My father started to get cereal from the cabinet.

"Wait!" I said.

"Wait what?" Dad asked.

"I'll get breakfast for you," I said.

Dad closed the cabinet door. "Well, thank you."

"How much will you pay me for getting your breakfast?"

"WHAT?" said Dad.

"Dad, I need a job."

Dad opened the cabinet door again. "I'll get my own cereal, thank you," said Dad.

I poured myself some cereal, too.

"Dad," I asked, "when you were my age, what did you do to make money?"

Dad leaned back in his chair. He looked up at the ceiling and smiled. Dad liked to think about the days when he was a boy.

"I used to deliver newspapers," he said, "but that was when I was older.

I used to collect empty bottles. I returned them to the store for the deposits. And I used to wash cars."

"Wash cars! What a great idea!" I said.

I started to run out of the house.

"Wait!" said Dad. "Your first job today is to put your spoon and bowl into the dishwasher — FREE OF CHARGE!"

Our neighbor, Mrs. Rizzo, lived by herself. She was happy when I offered to wash the car. "I usually take it to the car wash," she said. "But I hope you'll do a better job."

I helped my father wash his car many times, so I knew what to do. I wet the car with a hose. Then I filled a bucket with soapy water.

I washed every part: the doors, the hood, the trunk, the bumpers, the lights — even the wheels and the hubcaps. I had to jump up to reach the high parts.

Then I carried out Mrs. Rizzo's vacuum cleaner and vacuumed everything inside. I even vacuumed inside the trunk!

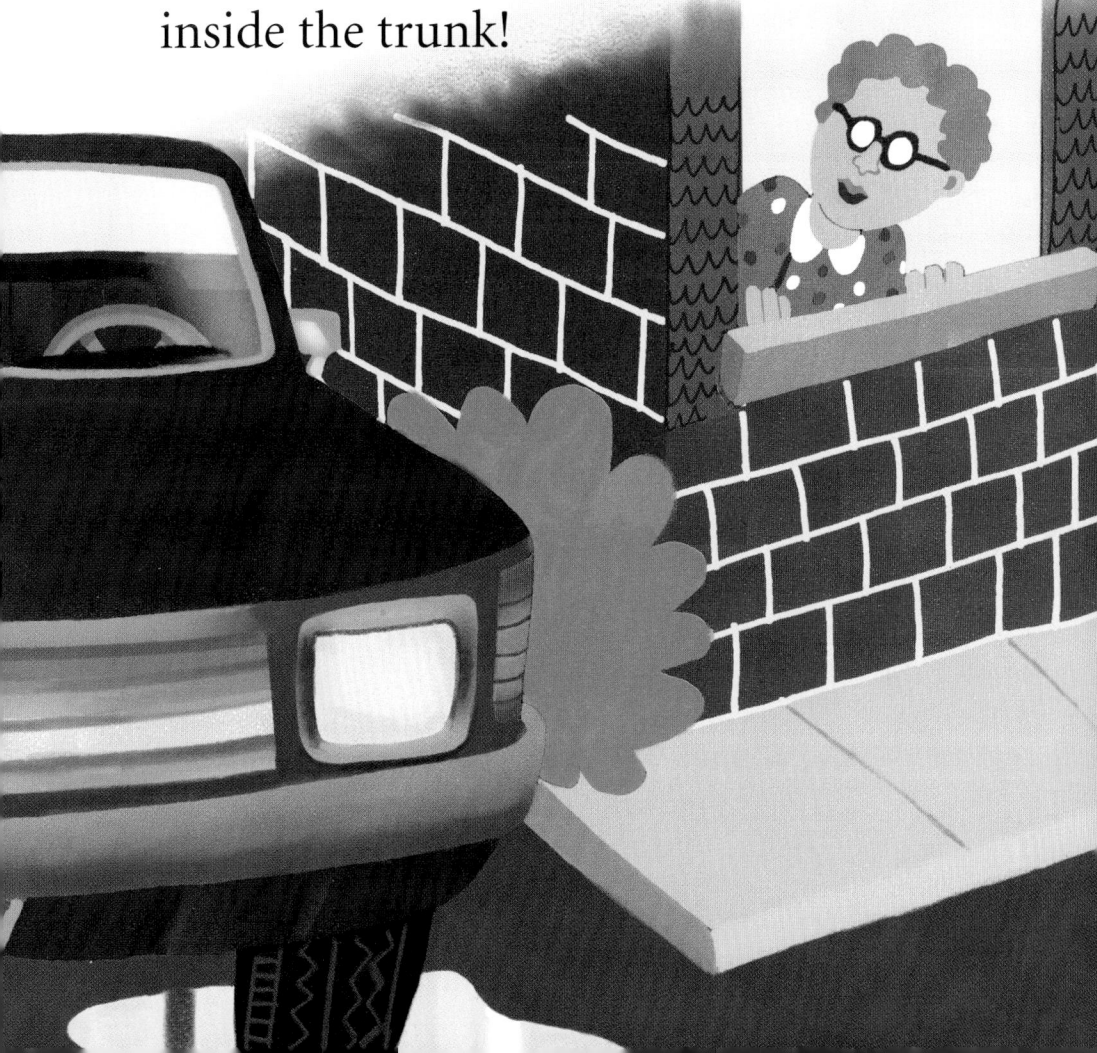

Mrs. Rizzo gave me rags for drying the car. I was tired, but the car looked pretty.

"It looks good," Mrs. Rizzo said. "Now you wax."

WAX?!!!

Waxing was even harder than washing. I put the wax on the car. Then I rubbed and rubbed. I had waxed half the car when Mrs. Rizzo gave me a peanut butter and jelly sandwich for lunch.

I finally finished waxing the car and Mrs. Rizzo gave me $5. Only $5? I was hoping for more. I should have set a price before starting.

Andrew and José walked by with a basketball. "Do you want to shoot some hoops?" Andrew asked.

I wanted to play, but I was too tired. "Later," I said, and I walked into my house. The clock said 3:15. I had worked almost all day, and I still needed $47.13!

Chapter Four

A soda can was on the table. I read the side of the label. "5¢ deposit!" I grabbed the can. Dad's voice boomed, "I'M DRINKING THAT!"

"Sorry, Dad," I said.

I waited for him to finish so I could have the can. You know, my father is the slowest soda drinker in the world.

"You need a haircut," said Mom. "Here's ten dollars. I want you to go to Mr. Yoshi and get your hair cut right now."

"But I have work to do," I said.

"Haircut first, work second," said Dad.

Dad put his empty can in a big plastic bag for me. Ready to start my next job, I went out the door. Collecting bottles and cans had to be easier than washing cars. But I had to get a haircut first.

On the way to Mr. Yoshi's shop,
I passed the school yard. I was in
luck. A soda can lay next to the goal
on the soccer field. I picked it up.
That's five cents, I said to myself.
I searched the rest of the field and
found more cans!

I saw another can next to a bush. I ran to get it. Zoom! It was gone. Behind the bush was a boy. He held two big bags. He must have had a hundred cans!

I ran to the playground to look for cans there. The boy ran to the handball courts. I found one can. The boy found a can, too. We both ran to the trash basket. I got there first.

I got to see the boy close-up. His clothes were dirty and torn. His shoes were worn-down and had holes. His eyes were kind of sad but they moved fast, looking for more cans.

That boy needed the cans more than I did. I left my cans next to the trash basket and walked away.

I walked over to the basketball courts. Andrew, José, Michael, and Fuchsia were there. "Are you ready to play?" Andrew asked. I still wanted to play. But I was supposed to get a haircut. And I still needed $47.13. Then I smiled. I had a great idea!

"Who knows how to cut hair?"

"I do," said Andrew.

"I'll give you two dollars to cut mine," I said.

I thought that I could spend two dollars on my haircut and keep eight dollars for my telescope!